MANGA MATH MYSTERIES

MATH

THE HUNDRED-DOLLAR ROBBER

A Mystery with Money

by Melinda Thielbar
illustrated by Tintin Pantoja

#2

GRAPHIC UNIVERSE™ • MINNEAPOLIS • NEW YORK

SAM
CARTER

AMY
TSANG

ADAM
BREGMAN

JOY
MEDINA

SIFU
FAIZA

MR. WATKINS

THE COLONIAL HEIGHTS SOCCER TEAM

STACY LOWICKI

TOM JOHNSON

KRISTIN

MIKE

We need math when we learn how to use **money.** We can add, subtract, multiply, and divide money. Sometimes we use **decimals** when writing amounts of money. For example, if we have $35.40, we have thirty-five dollars and forty cents. The decimal separates the dollars and cents.

When we add or subtract money, it is important to line up the decimals. If the amount does not have a decimal, we can add one. For example, if we add $2.45 and $3 we can add a decimal to $3. It should look like this:

$$\begin{array}{r} \$2.45 \\ +\$3.00 \\ \hline \$5.45 \end{array}$$

J-GN
MAGNA MATH
MYSTERIES
383-0935

Story by Melinda Thielbar
Pencils and inks by Tintin Pantoja
Coloring by Hi-Fi Design
Lettering by Marshall Dillon

Copyright © 2010 by Lerner Publishing Group, Inc.

Graphic Universe™ is a trademark of Lerner Publishing Group, Inc.

Graphic Universe™
A division of Lerner Publishing Group, Inc.
241 First Avenue North
Minneapolis, MN 55401 U.S.A.

Website address: www.lernerbooks.com

Library of Congress Cataloging-in-Publication Data

Thielbar, Melinda.
    The hundred-dollar robber : a mystery with money / by Melinda Thielbar ;
illustrated by Tintin Pantoja.
    p. cm. — (Manga math mysteries)
    Summary: Someone has stolen money from the soccer team's car-wash
earnings, and the students from Sifu Faiza's Kung Fu School must set aside their
feud with the soccer players to figure out how much money was stolen and by
whom.
    ISBN: 978-0-7613-3854-3 (lib. bdg. : alk. paper)
    1. Graphic novels. [1. Graphic novels. 2. Mystery and detective stories.
3. Mathematics—Fiction. 4. Kung fu—Fiction. 5. Schools—Fiction. 6. Soccer—
Fiction.] I. Pantoja, Tintin, ill. II. Title.
PZ7.7.T48Hu 2010
741.5'973—dc22   2008053709

Manufactured in the United States of America
1 2 3 4 5 6 – DP – 15 14 13 12 11 10

KEEP YOUR KNEES BENT. PUSH WITH YOUR FEET.

GOOD! DO IT AGAIN.

ADAM, ARE WE DONE YET?

THIRTY MORE SECONDS.

NOW TURN AROUND, BUT DON'T STRAIGHTEN YOUR KNEES.

PERFECT!

STACY, WAIT.

STACY SAID SHE WAS SORRY. SHE HELPED US GET OUR THINGS BACK.

STACY'S ASKING FOR OUR HELP. IF SIFU WERE HERE, WHAT WOULD SHE TELL US TO DO?

SHE'D SAY WE SHOULD ALWAYS HELP OTHERS WHEN WE CAN. EVEN TOM.

TELL US WHAT HAPPENED. WE'LL HELP IF WE CAN.

THANK YOU!

YESTERDAY, WE HAD A CAR WASH TO RAISE MONEY FOR THE SOCCER TEAM.

WE MADE OUR GOAL IN THE LAST FEW MINUTES.

COLONIAL HEIGHTS SOCCER FIELD

AFTER THE CAR WASH, WE WALKED BACK TO THE SOCCER FIELD.

TOM GOT INTO A FIGHT WITH THIS BOY NAMED MIKE.

HEY, TOM! I HEAR YOU'RE THE TEAM CHARITY CASE!

WHACK

TOM SAID HE WAS SICK AND HAD TO GO HOME, BUT WE ALL KNEW HE WAS JUST MAD.

I'M THE TEAM TREASURER. WHILE EVERYONE ELSE WAS PRACTICING, I COUNTED THE MONEY.

$100 WAS MISSING.

WE COUNTED TWICE, BUT THERE WAS ONLY $300 IN THE CASHBOX. WE THOUGHT WE COLLECTED $400.

EVERYONE WAS REALLY UPSET.

COACH SAID THERE WAS PROBABLY A MISTAKE AND WE SHOULD GO HOME.

KRISTIN, THE TEAM CAPTAIN, SAID IT WAS PRETTY OBVIOUS SOMEONE TOOK THE MONEY.

SHE SAID EVERYBODY SHOULD LET EVERYBODY ELSE LOOK IN THEIR STUFF. SHE LOOKED IN MY BAG TWICE.

NO ONE HAD THE MONEY, SO NOW EVERYONE THINKS TOM MUST HAVE TAKEN IT.

HOW DID YOU KNOW YOU SHOULD HAVE HAD $400?

WE GAVE EVERYONE A RECEIPT AND KEPT A COPY.

THIS IS THE RECEIPT BOOK WITH THE COPIES.

BESIDES, I KNOW THERE'S $100 MISSING EVEN WITHOUT COUNTING.

AT THE END OF THE DAY, KRISTIN'S NEIGHBOR GAVE US TWO $100 BILLS. THERE WAS ONLY ONE $100 BILL IN THE CASHBOX.

WE SHOULD MAKE SURE THE RECEIPTS ADD UP TO $400.

THE CAR WASH WAS BUSY. STACY MIGHT HAVE MADE A MISTAKE.

THERE'S 6 PAGES OF RECEIPTS. IT'LL TAKE *FOREVER* TO ADD UP.

YOU SAID ONE OF THE $100 BILLS WAS MISSING AND NONE OF THE PLAYERS HAD IT.

THAT'S RIGHT.

IF SOMEONE TOOK THE $100 BILL, MAYBE THEY SPENT IT ON THEIR WAY TO PRACTICE. MAYBE THEY DIDN'T HAVE IT ANYMORE WHEN YOU LOOKED IN EVERYONE'S BAGS.

MY MOM WORKS AT A FLOWER SHOP. THEY DON'T TAKE $100 BILLS BECAUSE IT USES UP ALL THEIR CHANGE IF YOU BUY SOMETHING SMALL WITH IT.

IF SOMEONE USED A HUNDRED DOLLAR BILL, THE PERSON AT THE STORE WOULD REMEMBER THEM.

THE SOCCER FIELD IS CLOSE TO THE CAR WASH. WE COULD ASK IN ALL THE STORES IN BETWEEN.

WAIT! WE'RE STILL GUESSING SOMEONE TOOK THE MONEY. MAYBE IT WAS JUST LOST.

WELL, WE COULD ALSO ASK IF SOMEONE FOUND A $100 BILL AND TURNED IT IN.

NICHOLS STREET ONLY HAS STORES ON ONE SIDE OF THE STREET. SEARCHING ONE BLOCK ON NICHOLS IS LIKE DOING HALF A BLOCK.

IT'S ALMOST THE SAME ON DANSKY AVENUE.

SO, ONE TEAM DOES KESSEL WAY, WHICH IS TWO BLOCKS, PLUS DANSKY AVENUE. THAT ADDS UP TO TWO AND A HALF BLOCKS.

THE OTHER TEAM DOES MAIN STREET, WHICH IS TWO BLOCKS, PLUS NICHOLS STREET. THAT MAKES TWO AND A HALF BLOCKS. THAT'S EVEN.

AND WHOEVER FINISHES FIRST CAN DO THE EXTRA HALF BLOCK OF DANSKY AVENUE.

ADAM, AMY, AND SAM, YOU BE TEAM 1. STACY AND I WILL BE TEAM 2.

THAT MAKES SENSE TO ME.

AYE AYE, CAP'N!

THE PERFECT CUP

SPECIAL ICED CARAM STEA $4.6

EXCUSE ME. I ASKED IF YOU WERE TALKING TO ME.

I'M AN ATHLETE. I WOULD NEVER DRINK THAT STUFF.

DON'T WORRY ABOUT IT, SAM.

BUT HER DRINK HAS *SWEET WHIPPED CREAM* ON IT, AND SHE SAYS *SODA* ISN'T GOOD FOR YOU!

AND ISN'T *CHOCOLATE* FULL OF SUGAR?!

SAM, REMEMBER WHAT SIFU SAYS ABOUT "BEING TRANQUIL IN SPIRIT."

I AM TRANQUIL IN SPIRIT.

OM...

BUT I'M *STILL MAD.*

YOU GUYS ARE BORING.

$3.50 Per Pound
+ .30 Tax Per Pound
$3.80 Total

SORRY, MISS, BUT DO YOU HAVE SOMETHING SMALLER?

THANKS! SOMEONE CAME IN YESTERDAY AND USED UP A LOT OF MY CHANGE. I HAVEN'T HAD TIME TO GO TO THE BANK FOR MORE.

THAT PERSON DIDN'T GIVE YOU A $100 BILL, DID THEY?

WHY, YES, I HAD TO GIVE $70 CHANGE: TWO FIVES, TWO TENS, AND TWO TWENTIES.

YOU CAN USE *DIVISION* TO FIND OUT HOW MUCH. IT COST $30, SO YOU DIVIDE $30 BY THE PRICE PER POUND.

BUT FIRST, WHY DO YOU NEED TO KNOW?

SOMEBODY STOLE A $100 BILL FROM A FRIEND OF OURS, AND WE THINK THEY SPENT IT HERE.

OH MY!

THE SIGN IS SMUDGED SO WE CAN'T READ HOW MUCH THE CANDY COST WITH TAX.

BUT WE KNOW THE PRICE IS $4.60, AND WE KNOW THE TAX IS $0.40. WE CAN ADD THEM TO FIND THE TOTAL.

$4.60 per pound
$ .40 tax per pound
$5.00 per pound with tax

YOU CAN ADD DECIMALS JUST LIKE WHOLE NUMBERS, BUT YOU HAVE TO MAKE SURE TO LINE UP THE DECIMAL POINTS.

I'LL ADD THE NUMBERS WITH THE CALCULATOR ON MY CELL PHONE, AND YOU DO IT ON PAPER.

IF WE GET THE SAME NUMBER, WE PROBABLY DID EVERYTHING RIGHT. IF WE GET DIFFERENT NUMBERS, ONE OF US MADE A MISTAKE AND WE'LL TRY AGAIN.

4.6

The price is
$5.00 per pound.

The person spent $30.00.
30 ÷ 5 is 6.
The person bought
6 pounds of candy.

SHE AND MIKE WERE AT TOM'S HOUSE TODAY TOO!

SOMETHING ELSE SEEMED STRANGE.

WHEN YOU GIVE SOMEONE $70 CHANGE, YOU USUALLY GIVE THEM 3 $20 BILLS AND ONE $10 BILL. BUT THEY WANTED 2 $5 BILLS, 2 $10 BILLS, AND 2 $20 BILLS.

$4.60 per pound
+$0.40 tax per pound
$5.00

The price is $5.00 per pound. The person spent $30.00. 30 ÷ 5 is 6. The person bought 6 pounds of candy.

THAT'S IT! I KNOW HOW THEY HID THE MONEY.

YOU BOUGHT THAT AT MR. WATKINS'S CANDY STORE.

I BET HE'LL RECOGNIZE YOU.

LOTS OF PEOPLE BUY CANDY.

BUT MOST OF THEM DON'T BUY A $30 BAG OF CANDY AND PAY WITH A $100 BILL.

IF I PAID $30 FOR A BAG OF CANDY, I WOULD GET $70 IN CHANGE. YOU CAN SEE THAT I DON'T HAVE IT.

YOU TOOK THE $100 BILL OUT OF THE CASHBOX.

YOU WERE AFRAID SOMEONE WOULD SEE YOU WITH A $100 BILL, SO YOU BOUGHT SOMETHING.

YOU GOT MR. WATKINS TO GIVE YOU YOUR CHANGE IN A STRANGE WAY. YOU ASKED FOR 2 $20 BILLS, 2 $10 BILLS, AND 2 $5 BILLS.

THAT WAY YOU COULD EACH TAKE EXACTLY HALF OF THE REMAINING MONEY. THAT GAVE YOU $35 EACH.

THE NEXT DAY . . .

SO, MIKE AND KRISTIN HAD TO GIVE THE MONEY BACK.

AND THE COACH AND THEIR PARENTS DECIDED THEY HAD TO WASH ENOUGH CARS TO PAY FOR MY TRIP TO THE TOURNAMENT AND FOR TOM'S.

YOU'RE STILL GOING?

THERE ARE 8 *NICE* PEOPLE ON THE TEAM WHO NEED US TO PLAY.

BUT AFTER THAT, I'M THROUGH WITH SOCCER.

WHAT ARE YOU GOING TO DO THEN?

I WAS THINKING I'D TRY KUNG FU.

The Author

Melinda Thielbar is a teacher who has written math courses for all ages, from kids to adults. In 2005 Melinda was awarded a VIGRE fellowship at North Carolina State University for PhD candidates "likely to make a strong contribution to education in mathematics." She lives in Raleigh, North Carolina, with her husband, author and video game programmer Richard Dansky, and their two cats.

The Artists

Tintin Pantoja was born in Manila in the Philippines. She received a degree in illustration and cartooning from the School of Visual Arts in New York City and was nominated for the Friends of Lulu "Best Newcomer" award. She was also a finalist in Tokyopop's Rising Stars of Manga 5. Her past books include a graphic novel version for kids of Shakespeare's play *Hamlet*.

Yuko Ota graduated from the Rochester Institute of Technology and lives in Maryland. She has worked as an animator and a lab assistant but is happiest drawing creatures and inventing worlds. She likes strong tea, the smell of new tires, and polydactyl cats (cats with extra toes!). She doesn't have any pets, but she has seven houseplants named Blue, Wolf, Charlene, Charlie, Roberto, Steven, and Doris.

Der-shing Helmer graduated with a degree in Biology from UC Berkeley, where she played with snakes and lizards all summer long. She is working toward becoming a biology teacher. When she is not tutoring kids, she likes to create art, especially comics. Her best friends are her two pet geckos (Smeg and Jerry), her king snake (Clarice), and the chinchilla that lives next door.

SAM BY TINTIN

START READING FROM THE OTHER SIDE OF THE BOOK!

This page would be the first page of a manga from Japan. This is because written Japanese is read from the right side of the page to the left side of the page. English is read from left to right, so this is the last page of this Manga Math Mystery. If you read the end of the book first, you'll spoil the mystery! Turn the book over so you can start on the first page. Then find the clues to the mystery with Sam, Joy, Amy, and Adam!

MANGA MATH MYSTERIES #3

Sam's little sister Michelle thinks there's a ghost in the creepy old house their dad bought. With help from a couple of friends on the soccer team, Sam, Amy, and Michelle use an old ghost story—plus measuring tools, distance, volume, and perimeters—to figure out the truth behind . . .

The Secret Ghost

MANGA MATH MYSTERIES

#1 THE LOST KEY A Mystery with Whole Numbers

#2 THE HUNDRED-DOLLAR ROBBER A Mystery with Money

#3 THE SECRET GHOST A Mystery with Distance and Measurement

#4 THE KUNG FU PUZZLE A Mystery with Time and Temperature